Modern
F

Illustrated by Leonard Shortall

The Boy
Who Would Not
Say His Name

ELIZABETH VREEKEN

MODERN CURRICULUM PRESS
Cleveland • Toronto

ISBN 0-8136-5541-2 Paperback
ISBN 0-8136-5041-0 Hardbound

9 10   99 98

Library of Congress Catalog Card Number: 59-8786

Bobby Brown was a boy who liked
to pretend.

Every day he would pretend to be
someone in a story.

One day he was Pinocchio.

One day he was Little Boy Blue.

Every day he had a different name.

One day Bobby crawled
into the kitchen.

"Look, Mother," he said.

"I am Timothy Turtle."

Mother laughed.

One day Bobby hopped
into the living room.

"Look, Daddy," he said.
"I am Peter Rabbit."

Daddy laughed.

But not everybody laughed.

Aunt Hilda called on the telephone.

Bobby answered.

"Is this Bobby?" asked Aunt Hilda.

"No," said Bobby.

"This is Little Jack Horner."

"Oh, I must have the wrong number,"
said Aunt Hilda.

Then she hung up.

Aunt Hilda was angry
when she found out it was Bobby.

One day Grandpa took Bobby
to the park.

They met an old friend.

"What is your name, little boy?"
asked the old friend.

"My name is Davy Crockett,"
said Bobby.

The old friend looked surprised.

Grandpa was angry at Bobby.

Daddy said, "This must stop.
It is not funny any more."

"Yes," said Mother. "Bobby must
learn to say his own name."

Bobby came in the room.

"What is your name?" asked Daddy.

"I am the Big Bad Wolf,"
said Bobby.

"Stop it," said Mother.
"You are Bobby. Bobby Brown.

Now say your name."

"I am the Big Bad Wolf," said Bobby.

"All right," said Mother.
"You can't read any more stories."

But still Bobby would not say

his name.

Daddy said to Mother,

"I will make him stop.

I have an idea."

Daddy called on the telephone.

Bobby answered it.

"Who is this?" asked Daddy.

"This is Peter Piper," said Bobby.

"Oh, that is too bad," said Daddy.

"I thought this was Bobby.

I want to take Bobby to the circus.

But I can't take Peter Piper."

Daddy hung up.

Still Bobby would not say his name.

Grandma said, "I have an idea.

I will make him stop."

The next day she brought a present.

The card on the present said FOR BOBBY.

"What is your name, little boy?"

Grandma asked.

"My name is Robin Hood," said Bobby.

"Oh, that is too bad," said Grandma.

"This present is for Bobby.

I can't give it to Robin Hood."

She took the present home.

Still Bobby would not say his name.

One day Bobby went to the store
with Mother.

It was a big store.

It was a busy store.

All of a sudden, Mother was gone.

Bobby looked and looked for her.

He called and called.

He could not find Mother.

A pretty lady came.

She took Bobby to a big room.

She said, "Don't worry, little boy.

We will find your mother."

Then she said,

"What is your name, little boy?"

"My name is Rumpelstiltskin,"
said Bobby.

"Rumpelstiltskin?" asked the lady.

"Yes," said Bobby.

"All right," said the lady.

"I will call for your mother."

She called into the loud speaker.

"Mrs. Stiltskin. Mrs. Stiltskin.

Please come to the third floor.

We have your little boy Rumpel."

Bobby and the lady waited.

Mother did not come.

The pretty lady called again.

"Mrs. Stiltskin, come and get Rumpel."

Still Mother did not come.

Then loud bells rang.

It was time to close the store.

"Come, Rumpel," said the lady.

"I will take you to the policemen.

They will help you find your mother."

Soon Bobby was with the policemen.

A big policeman gave Bobby his hat
to play with.

Then the big policeman said,
"Tell me your name, little boy.
Then we will call your mother."

"My name is Rumpelstiltskin."

"Rumpelstiltskin?" asked
the big policeman.

"Rumpelstiltskin," said Bobby.

The policeman got the telephone book.

He opened it.

He looked up and down.

He looked down and up. He said,
"There is no Stiltskin family here.

Is there a telephone in your house,
Rumpel?"

"Oh, yes," said Bobby.

The policeman opened the book again.

He looked and he looked.

"The Stiltskin family is not
in the telephone book," he said.

"Rumpel, you will just have
to stay here with us."

Bobby just sat there.

It was getting late.

Daddy was home now.

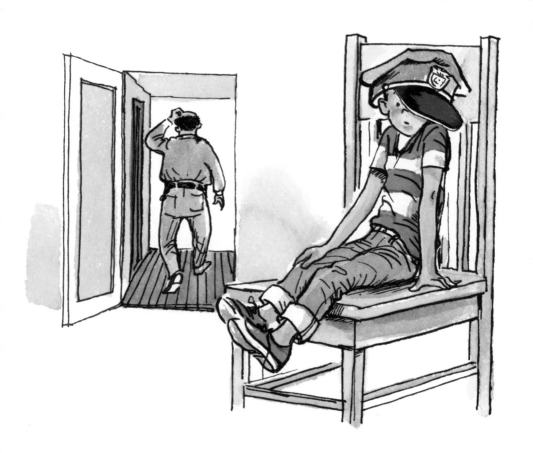

Mother was cooking a good dinner.

Bobby was hungry.

He was lonesome, too.

What if he had to stay there
all night?

What if he never got home again?

All at once he shouted,

"I am Bobby Brown!

　Bobby Brown is my name!

I am not Rumpelstiltskin.

　I am just Bobby Brown.

I live at 24 Third Street."

The big policeman looked in
the telephone book.

He found the Brown family.

He called Daddy on the telephone.

Soon Mother and Daddy came to
take Bobby home.

After that Bobby still liked
to pretend he was Pinocchio.

He liked to pretend he was
Robin Hood.

He liked to pretend he was
Peter Rabbit.

But when anyone asked him,
"What is your name?" he said,

"My name is Bobby Brown."

THE BOY WHO WOULD NOT SAY HIS NAME

The Boy Who Would Not Say His Name has a total vocabulary of 203 words. Regular plurals (*-s*) and regular verb forms (*-s, -ed, -ing*) of words already on the list are not listed separately, but the endings are given in parentheses after the words.

5	Bobby	in	said		Aunt
	Brown	story	I		Hilda
	was	one	am		call(ed)
	a	Pinocchio	Timothy		on
	boy	Little	Turtle		telephone
	who	Blue	laughed		answered
	liked	had	**7**	hopped	is
	to	different	living		this
	pretend	name	room		asked
	every	**6**	crawled	Daddy	**9**	no
	day	into	Peter		Jack
	he	the	Rabbit		Horner
	would	kitchen	**8**	but	oh
	be	look(ed)	not		must
	someone	Mother	everybody		have

wrong
number
then
she
hung
up
angry
when
found
out
it

10 Grandpa
took
park
they
met
an
old
friend
what
your

11 my
Davy
Crockett
surprised
at

12 stop
funny
any
more
yes
learn
say
his
own
came

13 Big
Bad
Wolf
you
are
now
all
right
can't
read
stories
still
would

14 will
make
him
idea

15 Peter
Piper
that
too
bad
thought
want
take
circus

16 Grandma
next
brought
present
card
for

17 Robin
Hood
give
home

18 went
store
with
busy
of
sudden
gone
and
her
could
find

19 pretty
lady
don't
worry
we

20 Rumpel-
stiltskin

21 loud
speaker
Mrs.
please
come
third
floor
waited
did
again
get
bells
rang
time
close

22 policemen
help
soon

policeman
gave
hat
play

23 tell
me

24 got
book
opened
down
there
family
here
house

25 just
stay
us
another
sat
getting
late

26 cooking
good
dinner
hungry
lonesome
if
night
never

27 once
shouted
live
24
Street

29 after
anyone